Dear Parents:

Congratulations! Your child is taking the first steps on an exciting journey. The destination? Independent reading!

STEP INTO READING® will help your child get there. The program offers five steps to reading success. Each step includes fun stories and colorful art or photographs. In addition to original fiction and books with favorite characters, there are Step into Reading Non-Fiction Readers, Phonics Readers and Boxed Sets, Sticker Readers, and Comic Readers—a complete literacy program with something to interest every child.

Learning to Read, Step by Step!

Ready to Read   Preschool–Kindergarten
• big type and easy words • rhyme and rhythm • picture clues
For children who know the alphabet and are eager to begin reading.

Reading with Help   Preschool–Grade 1
• basic vocabulary • short sentences • simple stories
For children who recognize familiar words and sound out new words with help.

Reading on Your Own   Grades 1–3
• engaging characters • easy-to-follow plots • popular topics
For children who are ready to read on their own.

Reading Paragraphs   Grades 2–3
• challenging vocabulary • short paragraphs • exciting stories
For newly independent readers who read simple sentences with confidence.

Ready for Chapters   Grades 2–4
• chapters • longer paragraphs • full-color art
For children who want to take the plunge into chapter books but still like colorful pictures.

STEP INTO READING® is designed to give every child a successful reading experience. The grade levels are only guides; children will progress through the steps at their own speed, developing confidence in their reading.

Remember, a lifetime love of reading starts with a single step!

Copyright © 2020 Disney Enterprises, Inc. and Pixar. All rights reserved. Published in
the United States by Random House Children's Books, a division of Penguin Random House LLC,
1745 Broadway, New York, NY 10019, and in Canada by Penguin Random House Canada
Limited, Toronto, in conjunction with Disney Enterprises, Inc.

Visit us on the Web!
StepIntoReading.com
rhcbooks.com

Educators and librarians, for a variety of teaching tools, visit us at RHTeachersLibrarians.com

ISBN 978-0-7364-3949-7 (trade)
ISBN 978-0-7364-8267-7 (lib. bdg.)
ISBN 978-0-7364-3950-3 (ebook)

Printed in the United States of America   10 9 8 7 6 5 4 3 2 1

DISNEY · PIXAR
ONWARD

Oh, Brother!

by Natasha Bouchard
illustrated by the Disney Storybook Art Team

Random House 🏠 New York

Ian and Barley

are brothers.

Ian is gentle.

Barley is rough.

Ian is quiet.

He does not

speak up.

Barley is loud.
Everyone
notices him.

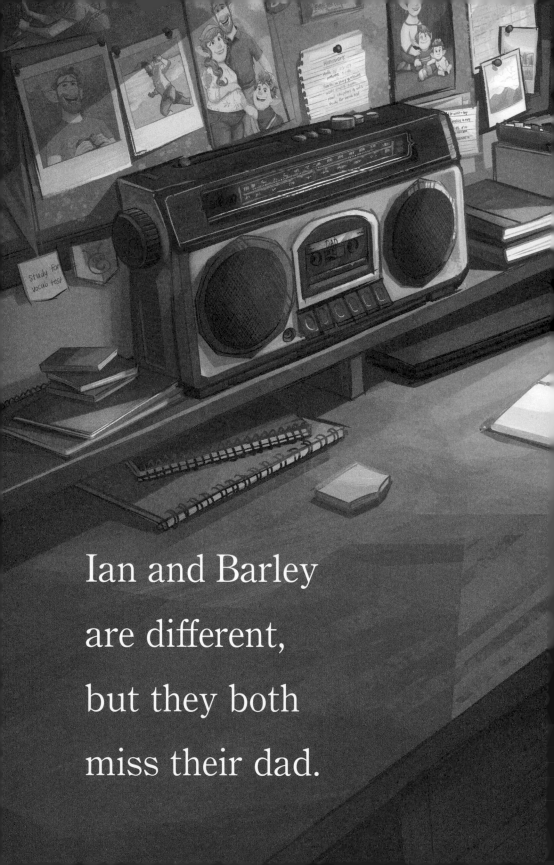

Ian and Barley
are different,
but they both
miss their dad.

Their dad left them
a special gift.
It is a magic spell!

Ian likes the
special gift.
But he does not
like magic.

Ian and Barley
try the spell.
Something goes wrong.
Only half of Dad
appears!

Ian and Barley must
finish the spell.
They need to find
a Phoenix Gem.

Ian does not think
the magic will work.
But Barley knows
it will.

The brothers arrive
at a scary place.
Barley wants be daring.
Ian wants to be safe.

Dad is in trouble!

Ian must act fast.

Ian saves Dad with magic!

Ian uses magic.
Ian is scared
to cross the pit.

Barley helps Ian
believe in himself.

The brothers
work together.
They make
a magic boat.

They find the
Phoenix Gem!
They finish
the spell.

Dad tells Barley
how proud he is
of his two sons.

Together,
the brothers
are stronger
than any magic.